FROM THE ATLANTIC TO THE PACIFIC:
CANADIAN EXPANSION
1867-1909

TITLE LIST

FROM THE ATLANTIC TO THE PACIFIC:
CANADIAN EXPANSION
1867-1909

BY
SHEILA NELSON

MASON CREST PUBLISHERS
PHILADELPHIA

Mason Crest Publishers Inc.
370 Reed Road
Broomall, Pennsylvania 19008
(866) MCP-BOOK (toll free)

First printing
1 2 3 4 5 6 7 8 9 10

Library of Congress Cataloging-in-Publication Data

Nelson, Sheila.
  From the Atlantic to the Pacific : Canadian expansion, 1867–1909 / by Sheila Nelson.
    p. cm. — (How Canada became Canada)
  Includes index.
  ISBN 1-4222-0005-1   ISBN 1-4222-0000-0 (series)
  1. Frontier and pioneer life—Canada, Western—Juvenile literature. 2. Canada—History—1867—Juvenile literature. 3. Canada—Territorial expansion—Juvenile literature. 4. Canada, Western—History—Juvenile literature. I. Title.
  F1033.N43 2006
  971.05—dc22
                              2005010698

Produced by Harding House Publishing Service, Inc.
www.hardinghousepages.com
Interior design by MK Bassett-Harvey.
Cover design by Dianne Hodack.
Printed in the Hashemite Kingdom of Jordan.

CONTENTS

INTRODUCTION

by David Bercuson

Every country's history is distinct, and so is Canada's. Although Canada is often said to be a pale imitation of the United States, it has a unique history that has created a modern North American nation on its own path to democracy and social justice. This series explains how that happened.

Canada's history is rooted in its climate, its geography, and in its separate political development. Virtually all of Canada experiences long, dark, and very cold winters with copious amounts of snowfall. Canada also spans several distinct geographic regions, from the rugged western mountain ranges on the Pacific coast to the forested lowlands of the St. Lawrence River Valley and the Atlantic tidewater region.

Canada's regional divisions were complicated by the British conquest of New France at the end of the Seven Years' War in 1763. Although Britain defeated France, the French were far more numerous in Canada than the British. Britain was thus forced to recognize French Canadian rights to their own language, religion, and culture. That recognition is now enshrined in the Canadian Constitution. It has made Canada a democracy that values group rights alongside individual rights, with official French/English bilingualism as a key part of the Canadian character.

During the American Revolution, Canadians chose to stay British. After the Revolution, they provided refuge to tens of thousands of Americans who, for one reason or another, did not follow George Washington, Benjamin Franklin, or the other founders of the United States who broke with Britain.

Democracy in Canada under the British Crown evolved more slowly than it did in the United States. But in the early nineteenth century, slavery was outlawed in the

British Empire, and as a result, also in Canada. Thus Canada never experienced civil war or government-imposed racial segregation.

From these few, brief examples, it is clear that Canada's history differs considerably from that of the United States. And yet today, Canada is a true North American democracy in its own right. Canadians will profit from a better understanding of how their country was shaped—and Americans may learn much about their own country by studying the story of Canada.

Early settlers arriving at the Red River Colony

One

THE BIRTH OF THE WEST

In the Red River Colony, on the wide prairie west of the Great Lakes, the Métis—descended from the children of French fur traders and *First Nations* women—lived side by side with English and Scottish settlers in an uneasy peace. The Métis, French-speaking Roman Catholics, outnumbered the English-speaking Protestants.

To the east, Canada had become a country when *confederation* joined the provinces of Québec, Ontario, New Brunswick, and Nova Scotia under one government. Now Canada looked west, to Rupert's Land, the vast wilderness area owned by the Hudson's Bay Company (the HBC). Apart from the Red River Colony, few Europeans lived there; all Canada would have to do was negotiate a purchase.

The English and Scottish settlers liked the idea of joining Canada, but the Métis were not so sure. Many First Nations people in North America had lost their land and their rights when the Europeans arrived. Joining Canada would mean many more Canadians would flow into the Red River area. The Métis wondered if they would be able to keep their land and their traditions amid all these changes.

First Nations is the term Canadians use to represent their native population.

A confederation is a group of aligned or united states.

9

Annexing means taking control over territory and incorporating it into another political entity.

Expansion

In 1867, the United States purchased Alaska from Russia. The purchase alarmed many Canadians, and they worried the United States would try and take over more northern and western territory. People in British Columbia were especially nervous. British Columbians were interested in joining the confederation of Canada, but thousands of miles separated them from the eastern provinces. Now, with American land to both their north and their south, they felt pressured by the United States and isolated from Canada. Americans—and some British Columbians—began to talk about *annexing* British Columbia to the United States.

Canada wanted to make sure the United States would not be able to gain any more northern or western land. Prime Minister John A. Macdonald decided the best way to keep the Americans out was to buy Rupert's Land and the North-Western Territory from the Hudson's Bay Company—the HBC—and to populate the west with Canadian settlers. A group of Canadian politicians traveled to Great Britain to negotiate a purchase.

In 1869, Canada finalized the purchase agreements with the HBC. On December 1, 1869, Canada would take control of Rupert's Land and the North-Western Territory. The HBC would continue to control their trading forts, however, along with the land around them.

Unrest at Red River

In 1868, a young man named Louis Riel returned from Canada to the Red River Colony (part of Rupert's Land),

John A. Macdonald

An HBC trading post

Separatists in Nova Scotia

Canada had been a country only a few months when anti-Confederationists in Nova Scotia started petitioning Great Britain to allow their province to secede from the rest of Canada. Joseph Howe, the leader of the anti-Confederation movement, had tried to block Nova Scotia's participation in Confederation before the British North America Act had gone into effect on July 1, 1867. The premier, Charles Tupper, had been a strong supporter of Confederation. Tupper had gone ahead and signed the act in spite of Howe's protests and the objections of many Nova Scotians. In February of 1868, Howe sent a petition to London to ask that Nova Scotia's part in the British North America Act be repealed. Nova Scotians wanted to be able to trade with the United States without any limits set by the Canadian government. After much negotiation, Howe finally gave up the fight for separation. In return, Nova Scotia would receive more money each year from the federal government.

where he had been studying and working. Riel had been born into a Métis family in Red River and had left to go to school in Montréal when he was thirteen years old.

When Riel arrived in Red River, he discovered the colony had changed in the time he had been away. More English-speaking English and Scottish settlers had arrived, and the English settlement at Fort Garry—

later renamed Winnipeg—was growing and thriving. The colony had become sharply divided between the English-speaking Protestants and the French-speaking Catholics.

Soon after Riel's arrival, news reached Red River of Canada's plans to purchase Rupert's Land and the North-Western Territory. Most of the English-speaking peo-

Early Red River settlers included many nationalities. This sketch shows a Swiss family, a Scots Highlander, a German, and a French Canadian.

ple in the colony were pleased at the thought of joining Canada, but the Métis were alarmed. Nobody had asked them if they wanted to be a part of Canada.

In the fall of 1868, a road-building crew arrived in Red River in preparation for the Canadian annexation of the area. Charles Mair, a Canadian poet, came with the work crew. The Canadian government had com-

missioned him to write a series of articles on Red River for Ontario newspapers, intended to attract settlers to the region. Mair's articles were very critical of the Métis. He wrote about the many "half-breeds" in Red River and recommended bringing in large groups of English-speaking Canadian settlers to dilute the Métis influence. In response, Louis Riel wrote articles for a Montreal newspaper defending the Métis. Riel also mocked Mair's glowing descriptions of the climate and land at Red River. He did not want settlers rushing to settle in the west after reading Mair's articles.

In the summer of 1869, before the HBC had even transferred the land to Canada, Canadian surveyors arrived and started drawing up maps, marking out lots for new settlers. The lots would be square, in the English and American style, unlike the long, narrow French-style lots of the Métis residents. The leader of the survey team had been told to leave the Métis land alone, but some boundary lines were ignored anyway. The Métis were now becoming angry, as they saw their rights overlooked by the Canadians. In August, Riel stood on the steps of the Catholic Cathedral and condemned the survey, calling it a menace to the Métis people.

Louis Riel

William McDougall

Fighting for Métis Rights

Despite the protests of the Métis, the survey continued. Finally, on October 11, Riel and a group of sixteen Métis walked up to the surveyors and stopped their work. After that, the Métis began to work politically to represent their own interests. Riel organized the National Committee to unite the Métis and prevent Canada from taking over Red River until the Canadian government had agreed to respect Métis rights.

Prime Minister Macdonald had appointed William McDougall to be the new governor of Rupert's Land and the North-Western Territory when they became a part of Canada. McDougall did not like the French or the Métis. While Riel and the Métis were forming the National Committee, McDougall was traveling to Red River to take up his position as governor. Since roads had not yet been built north of the Great Lakes linking Red River with Canada, McDougall traveled through the United States.

When the Métis heard McDougall had crossed the border into Canada, they marched out to meet him. On November 2, 1869, McDougall and his party were met by a group of armed Métis who ordered them to turn back. When McDougall left, the Métis took control of Fort Garry, the capital of Red River.

Riel tried to unite the English- and French-speaking people in the colony. He invited the English and Scottish settlers to send *delegates* to a convention with the Métis, so all the people of Red River could decide their future together. He believed Red River should enter Canada on its own terms, instead of having everything decided for it by far-away politicians.

The Canadians had not expected to face any problems in taking control of Red River—although the governor and

Delegates are people chosen to represent or act on behalf of others.

Cuthbert Grant, a Métis leader

***Anarchy** is a total lack of government and control.*

*If something is **provisional**, it is temporary, lasting only until it is replaced.*

priests of the colony had warned them the Métis would not be pleased. Because of the continuing troubles in Red River, Macdonald indefinitely postponed the date Canada would take control of the huge northwestern territories from the HBC.

On December 1, 1869, the day Canada was to have gained power of the region, the HBC gave up control. Red River was now essentially independent, ruled by no one. This was a dangerous position for the settlers. They were now governed by no laws and protected by no army. To prevent *anarchy* and

Portage la Prairie

chaos, the Métis and other settlers quickly formed a *provisional* government to rule until the future of the colony was decided.

Around the same time, a group of Canadian soldiers arrived to arrest Riel because he was stirring up rebellion and keeping McDougall, the new governor, out of Red River. McDougall claimed Riel was a traitor to Britain and was working with the Americans to steal land from Canada. Riel denied the accusation. He was loyal to the Queen and Great Britain, he said, but he wanted what was best for his people. Before the Canadian soldiers could act, Riel had them surrounded and thrown into prison at Fort Garry.

During the winter of 1869 and 1870, the provisional government, under Louis Riel, worked with the Canadian government to define the terms under which Red River would enter Canada. Riel had written a List of Rights he wanted included before Red River would agree to join Canada. The List of Rights included the right of representation in Canadian parliament and the guarantee that the new provincial government would be bilingual. Most of the people Macdonald sent to Red River to negotiate agreed the List of Rights was reasonable and fair. In February, Riel freed all the prisoners he had captured in December—although three had already escaped. The residents of

The execution of Thomas Scott

Red River started to relax; the unrest of the last year seemed to be fading.

The Execution of Thomas Scott

The three prisoners who had escaped from Fort Garry in January had been busy. They had gone to Portage la Prairie, southwest of Fort Garry along the American border, to raise support for an attack on Riel. One of the men was Thomas Scott, an Irish Protestant who did not like the Métis. In Portage la Prairie, Scott told wild stories about the horrible conditions in prison and the terrible way Riel and the Métis had treated him.

The men convinced Captain Charles Boulton to lead the attack on Fort Garry. Forty-eight Canadians marched from Portage la Prairie toward Fort Garry, intent on freeing the prisoners. When they learned the prisoners had already been released, most of the men were ready to go home—but Scott and his two friends wanted to continue the attack. Captain Boulton realized they had never really cared about freeing the prisoners; they wanted to capture Riel and take over the provisional government in Red River.

Boulton and his men started to go home to Portage la Prairie, but they traveled close to Fort Garry on the way. The men of the fort came out to protect themselves and captured almost all the Canadians. Riel ordered that Boulton be executed. The execution would serve as an example to the rest of

Canada; Riel was tired of the Canadians thinking they could just march in and take over. The Canadian negotiators in Red River pleaded with Riel to pardon Boulton, and finally Riel agreed.

The troubles might have ended with Boulton's pardon, but for Thomas Scott. Scott insulted his Métis guards continually, starting fights and calling them cowards and half-breeds. Scott angered the Métis so much that when he was tried, they sentenced him to death. No amount of appeals would change Riel's mind this time. On March 4, 1870, Scott was executed by a firing squad.

A settler's home in Manitoba

Parliament building in Ottawa

In Red River, life went back to normal, and the provisional government worked out the final agreements for joining Canada. Back in Ontario, though, people suddenly became aware of the events in Red River. Scott had been a member of the Orangemen, a *fraternal organization* of Protestants. The Orangemen hated Catholics, and the Métis were Catholics. Scott became a hero to his fellow Orangemen, a great man who had been murdered by the evil Riel.

*A **fraternal organization** is a group composed of male members with similar goals and beliefs.*

Settlers to Manitoba

British Columbia's wild mountains

Manitoba Joins Canada

On July 15, 1870, the Manitoba Act finally gave Canada control of Rupert's Land and the North-Western Territory. On the same day, the Red River Colony became the province of Manitoba, much smaller than the Manitoba of today. At the time, Cana-dians called it the "postage stamp province" because of its size. The new province had been given the rights Riel had fought for—representation, bilingualism, and the right to teach their children in Catholic schools.

Meeting in Ottawa to sign the Manitoba Act, delegates from Red River agreed a military force would travel to the new province to oversee the transfer of power from the provisional government. Prime Minister Macdonald wanted to be sure the Métis would not try to make any last-minute trouble. Although the mission was officially peaceful, many of the men were young Orangemen, ready to kill Riel and avenge the death of Thomas Scott. The journey took three months, traveling across the Great Lakes and along rivers.

Riel heard about the approaching forces before they arrived. Fearing for his life, he escaped across the border into the United States. "The rights of the Métis are assured by the Manitoba Bill," he told a friend before he left. "It is what I wanted; my mission is finished."

Macdonald and the Canadian government had not expected to face so many problems in trying to purchase the huge northwestern territories from the HBC. Finally, nearly a year after they had hoped, Rupert's Land and the North-Western Territory—together now called the Northwest Territories—belonged to Canada. In the process, the new province of Manitoba had joined Confederation.

Now, British Columbia was no longer geographically separated from Canada, although it was still isolated from the distant Canadian cities. On July 20, 1871, British Columbia joined Canada after Prime Minister Macdonald's promise to build a cross-continental railway system. The railway would link the new province with the rest of Canada.

At the time of Confederation in 1867, Canada had consisted of four provinces on the east side of the continent. Now, only four years later, Canada reached from the Atlantic to the Pacific, its original size doubled many times over. With the new land came new issues to face. The First Nations people had never been consulted about the creation of Canada and the reorganization of territory. They had no Louis Riel, well-educated in Canadian schools and passionate about their cause, to speak for them and make sure their rights were protected.

The Saskatchewan River brought settlers into the western lands.

Two
CLAIMING THE WEST

As the morning of June 1, 1873, wore on, the men began to wake up. They had camped near one of the whiskey trading posts on the southern Canadian prairies and had spent the previous night drinking heavily. Most of them were still drunk as they roused themselves and started drinking again. The men were "wolfers." They looked for the carcasses of buffalo, skinned and left by robe makers, and sprinkled poison on the buffalo meat. Then they sat back and waited for hungry wolves to eat the meat and die, so they could take the wolf skins. Unfortunately, other animals, and sometimes people, also ate the buffalo meat and died.

The wolfers had crossed the American border into Canada, entering the Cypress Hills region of what is now Saskatchewan, looking for some stolen horses. A group of Assiniboine had camped nearby, but the men at the whiskey fort had told the wolfers the Assiniboine had not stolen their horses. When the wolfers woke up, however, one noticed his horse was missing. He was convinced the Assiniboine had taken it.

The men drank a little more whiskey and then marched over to the Assiniboine camp to take back their horse. Before they reached the camp, they came across the missing animal, but by that time they didn't care. They wanted a fight. They strode into camp and opened fire. In the fighting, twenty-two Assiniboine and one wolfer were killed; clearly, the Canadian west was not always a peaceful place.

The Numbered Treaties

The Canadian government wanted to fill the west with settlers. This, they believed, was the best way to make sure the United States was not able to take over western Canadian territory. However, most of the land still be-

longed to the First Nations people. The Royal Proclamation of 1763, issued soon after Great Britain had gained control of Canada, had guaranteed the First Nations rights to all land west of the settled eastern regions. Canada had purchased the Northwest Territories from the HBC, but that did not mean the country was free to sell off pieces of the land to settlers. First, Canada had to negotiate treaties with the First Nations tribes who lived on the land.

In 1871, the government began acquiring western land from the First Nations. During

the 1870s, seven treaties were signed with various First Nations of the Plains. The treaties gave the Canadian government the right to bring settlers out to the west and legally sell them land. In return, the First Nations who signed the treaties would be given money and reserve land to live on. The Canadian government would also build schools on the reserves, provide farm tools and animals, and stop the sale of alcohol to First Nations people. Some treaties stated that the Canadian government would supply food and medicine when needed as well. This series of seven treaties in the 1870s—together with another four in the next several decades—was called the Numbered Treaties; each treaty was simply named according to number, such as Treaty Number One or Treaty Number Four.

Some First Nations chiefs did not want to sign the treaties. They did not see why they should give up their land. Although some

First Nations people depended on the land and nature for their way of life.

27

held out longer than others, they eventually gave in as they saw their traditional way of life crumbling. The buffalo herds roaming the prairies had shrunk, and food was scarce. The treaties became the only way to save their people.

Dividing Up the Land

As soon as the Canadian government had gotten the land from the First Nations, they began dividing it into lots to sell to settlers. The Dominion Lands Survey started in July

What Did the Numbered Treaties Give the First Nations?

The eleven Numbered Treaties each gave similar things to the First Nations who signed them. Treaties Number One, Two, and Five provided 160 acres (64.75 hectares) of reserve land for each family of five, while the other treaties gave one square mile (2.5 square kilometers) of reserve land to each family. Most treaties paid a certain amount each year for every person living on the reserve—usually five dollars per person plus twenty-five dollars for each chief. Regular censuses would ensure the First Nations would receive the right amount of money. The Canadian government would build schools on reserve land when the First Nations asked for them and would give the Native people farming tools and, in some cases, fishing supplies and ammunition. Terms of the treaties usually allowed First Nations people the right to hunt and fish on the land they had given up to the Canadian government, as long as the land was unoccupied.

Early settlers in the Canadian west built sod homes.

of 1871. The surveyors measured and mapped the prairie land, marking out property lines and roads. Each township had thirty-six one-square-mile sections; each section was then divided into four 160-acre (64.75-hectare) plots.

In 1872, Canada passed the Dominion Lands Act. Under the Dominion Lands Act, men who were at least twenty-one years old could pay a ten-dollar registration fee for the title to one 160-acre (64.75-hectare) section of land. The settlers had three years to build a house on the land and start farming. If they met that requirement, the land was theirs to keep for free. Only every other lot was sold at first, so that settlers could have the opportunity to extend their claim into the empty sections next to their lots.

Canada was hoping for a huge rush of pioneers moving toward the west, building houses and laying out farms on their plots of land. Some people were tempted by the free land offered by the Dominion Lands Act, but far fewer than politicians had expected. The railway Canada intended to build across the country had been given nearly half the available land. Settlers who wanted to take advantage of the free land would have to build their farms twenty miles (32 kilometers) away from the soon-to-be-built railway. Another twenty years would pass before Canada saw a large number of settlers flow into the west.

The North West Mounted Police

In June of 1873, the group of American wolfers crossed the border into Canada and killed twenty-two Assiniboine men, women,

The North-Western Territories' rugged terrain

and children. When Canadians heard about the Cypress Hills Massacre, they were outraged. The Americans had crossed the border as though it did not exist. To Canadians, this meant Americans did not respect Canada's *sovereignty*.

The violence of the massacre also angered Canadians. Settlers were traveling west, and they were unprotected from such attacks. Prime Minister Macdonald had just created a police force, the North West Mounted Police—the NWMP— to patrol the Northwest Territories, especially along the border with the United States where people were beginning to

Sovereignty means independence, self-rule.

31

settle. The timing of the Cypress Hills Massacre only reinforced the need for a western police force.

One of the NWMP's first jobs was to get rid of the whiskey forts. American whiskey traders had built many of these forts, but treaties with the First Nations had promised to stop the sale of alcohol to Native people. The liquor sold at these forts could hardly even have been termed whiskey. Traders mixed the alcohol themselves, adding special ingredients such as chewing tobacco, red peppers, and soap. People sometimes died from drinking the brew.

The NWMP did not have a difficult time putting an end to the whiskey trade. Their presence in the area was enough to make most traders shut down their businesses and leave their forts. From far across the prairie, the traders could see the bright red

jackets of the NWMP (designed to distinguish them from the blue uniforms of the American military); almost no one stayed for the confrontation.

With the Numbered Treaties, Canada gained land to sell to western settlers, and with the Dominion Lands Act, the settlers gained free farm land. The NWMP—later to be renamed the RCMP, the Royal Canadian Mounted Police—assured the safety of the settlers and of the railway men who would soon begin building the cross-Canada railway. Before the building of the railway could begin, however, private companies would compete for the construction contract. This competition would lead to a scandal that would rock the Canadian government at its very highest level.

The NWMP drilling outside their barracks in Saskatchewan

The coming of the railway to the Canadian west

Three
SCANDALS AND CHANGES

Lucius Seth Huntington, the Member of Parliament from Shefford County, Québec, stood and addressed the House of Commons. "I demand a council of inquiry!" Huntington declared.

Before the last election, Huntington stated, certain high-ranking government members received large amounts of money from Sir Hugh Allan and the Canadian Pacific Railway Company. In return, Prime Minister Sir John A. Macdonald had promised to give Allan's company the contract to build the cross-Canada railway. This was blatant bribery.

Macdonald did not appear bothered by the accusation. He called for a vote on the proposed council of inquiry. The proposal was voted down.

The Pacific Scandal

Huntington first mentioned bribery for the railway contract in the House of Commons on April 2, 1873. Macdonald and the Conservative Party had won the election of 1872, but it was a hard-fought and difficult win. Political campaigns were expensive. The Canadian people were scattered across a wide area, many isolated in small, hard-to-reach settlements. Communications were slow, but campaigning meant somehow getting in touch with as many Canadians as possible. It also meant making sure voters could get to the polls to vote.

Ethical means conforming to agreed principles of moral conduct.

Macdonald knew money was needed to win votes, so he borrowed from as many friends and supporters as he could. One of these supporters was Sir Hugh Allan. Since Allan ran one of the railway companies competing for the cross-Canada railway contract, this financial support was hardly *ethical*.

Prince Edward Island's fertile farmland

In the summer of 1872, Macdonald discovered that his friend and political partner Sir George-Étienne Cartier had promised Allan the railway contract in exchange for $350,000 to be used toward election expenses, a huge amount at the time. Macdonald was shocked at how much money Allan had donated, but he accepted Cartier's promise and awarded Allan the contract.

Almost no one knew about Allan's financial gifts to Macdonald and the Conservative Party until Huntington accused the prime minister in the House of Commons in the spring of 1873. After the accusation, Macdonald continued to deny any bribery

Prince Edward Island Joins Canada

In 1871, the government of Prince Edward Island started construction on a railway line. The cost of construction was very high. Government debts mounted, threatening the colony with bankruptcy. Although Prince Edward Island had rejected Confederation with Canada in the past, in 1873, its government opened negotiations with Prime Minister Macdonald. Macdonald promised to take over the island's debts. On July 1, 1873, Prince Edward Island joined Canada, becoming the seventh province.

Sir George-Étienne Cartier

or wrongdoing, but even his own party members had become suspicious.

In July, newspapers suddenly published a copy of a telegram sent from Prime Minister Macdonald to Sir Hugh Allan. "I must have another $10,000," the telegram read. "Will be the last time of calling. Do not fail me. Answer today." Macdonald could no longer deny he had taken large amounts of money from Allan.

Macdonald tried to explain to the governor general—the Queen's representative in Canada—how much money elections and campaigns cost. Donations and loans from private businesspeople were needed to win an election. The problem was not with taking donations in general, however; Macdonald's problem was that he had taken money from someone trying to win a government contract. Worse, he had agreed to award Allan the railway contract in exchange for the money.

Some Canadians were less bothered by Allan's buying the railway contract than by where Allan got his money. Allan had many American backers. Canadians did not like the American interest in the Canadian railway.

After the publication of Macdonald's telegram to Allan, *Conservative* politicians began to abandon the party. They wanted to distance themselves from the scandal as

General Elections

In Canada, a general election does not directly elect the prime minister. Instead, each voting district (called "ridings") elects a representative to Parliament. The leader of the party that gets the most parliamentary seats then becomes prime minister.

much as possible. Macdonald tried to hold his party together, but the stress began to wear away at him. He had always had an alcohol problem, but now he started drinking heavily. By fall, the Conservatives had lost so many politicians that the Members of Parliament called a vote of no confidence in the House of Commons. On November 7, 1873, Macdonald and his government resigned.

*Someone who is **conservative** favors traditional views and values.*

*The **majority party** is the political party with the most members in government.*

Alexander Mackenzie

Just before Macdonald and the Conservatives left power late in 1873, the governor general began searching quickly for a replacement prime minister to lead the country. The governor general had the responsibility of making sure Canada always had a prime minister, usually by asking a Member of Parliament from the *majority party* to serve in that position until an election could be called. At first, the governor general

The Royal Military College of Canada

40

John A. Macdonald

*Something that is **interim** is temporary.*

Alexander Mackenzie

had trouble finding someone. Finally, the fourth person he asked, Alexander Mackenzie of the Liberal Party, agreed to become ***interim*** prime minister.

Alexander Mackenzie became the second prime minister of Canada on the same day Macdonald left office. In January

41

1874, Canada held a general election to officially choose a new prime minister. Tired of the Conservative Party and the Pacific Railway scandal, the Canadian people wanted change. The Liberal Party swept the election, winning 63 percent of the seats and confirming Alexander Mackenzie as prime minister.

Mackenzie was a Scottish immigrant who had worked as a stonemason, a building contractor, and a newspaper editor after coming to Canada, until he had entered politics as a Member of Parliament. He had a reputation for honesty and hard work that Canadians respected. He strongly believed in democracy and equality; from experience, he knew a person could rise from a low position to a very high one.

During Mackenzie's time as prime minister of Canada, he made several important reforms. The first of these was the secret ballot in 1874. Before Mackenzie introduced the secret ballot, voters had to publicly state whom they were voting for. That system easily allowed people to bully or intimidate others into voting for certain candidates.

Mackenzie also created the Supreme Court of Canada in 1875 (although Sir John A. Macdonald had earlier worked to establish such a court). The Supreme Court presided over all the other courts in the country. People who lost a case in a lower court could appeal the decision in the Supreme Court.

Other government changes brought about by Prime Minister Mackenzie included the Office of the Auditor General, to watch over government spending; the Department of Militia and Defence, to protect the country; and the Royal Military College of Canada, to train military leaders.

Working on the Railway

Prime Minister Macdonald had allowed private companies to compete for the contract to build the cross-Canada railway. When the Pacific scandal broke and Macdonald left office, plans for the railway were put on hold. Mackenzie was not as excited about the railway as Macdonald had been. He wanted to put off the project altogether, but British Columbia had been promised a railway when they joined Canada in 1871. Mackenzie thought building such an extensive railway as quickly as Macdonald had promised was crazy, and the cost would be much too high.

Mackenzie tried to find a Canadian company to finance the railway construction, but the economy had just entered a *depression*, and no one wanted to risk their money. Several American railway companies had recently gone bankrupt, and businesspeople did not want to face the same problem. With no available private financing, Mackenzie chose to have the government build the railway a little at a time, as money became available. The people of British Columbia did not like this solution at all. Macdonald had promised them a railway would be completed by 1881, but Mackenzie's style of building meant the project would take much longer to complete.

British Columbia sent a group to talk to Mackenzie about their concerns. If they did not get their railway quickly, the members of the delegation warned, British Columbia would separate from Canada and run its own affairs. Mackenzie was not interested in listening to such threats. Frustrated at the lack of response from the prime minister, the delegation went to the governor general to ask him to negotiate with Mackenzie.

*A **depression** is a period of slow economic activity with high unemployment.*

The rail line crossed the Canadian Rockies.

A political cartoon portrays Mackenzie with Lord Dufferin.

The governor general of Canada at the time was Lord Dufferin, a skilled diplomat. Without consulting Mackenzie, Lord Dufferin convinced the British Columbians not to leave Canada. In return, British Columbia would receive an annual payment until the railway was completed.

Mackenzie was not happy with Lord Dufferin for going behind his back to deal with the British Columbia situation. As governor general, Lord Dufferin technically had power over the prime minister, but his position was mainly symbolic. The expectation was that the governor general would not act on his own but would simply confirm the actions of the prime minister. Nevertheless, Lord Dufferin's actions ensured the unity of Canada.

The National Policy

During Mackenzie's time as prime minister, Canada's economy weakened. Mackenzie tried to organize a *free trade* agreement with the United States, but it failed. The United States had very high *tariffs* on imported goods, which most Canadians could not afford to pay. Canada had tariffs as well, but they were much lower than those in the United States. American businesspeople could easily bring their surplus goods into Canada and sell them cheaply. In this way, they could keep the prices of Canadian goods high in the United States, which hurt Canadian manufacturers. Meanwhile, cheap goods from the United States were brought

Laying the railroad across the west

into Canada, creating competition for Canadian manufacturers.

In 1878, Canada held a general election. Mackenzie's campaign platform centered on a free trade deal with the United States. Sir John A. Macdonald ran against Mackenzie, taking the exact opposite stance. He introduced a program he called

Free trade means few restrictions of trade practices.

Tariffs are taxes on imported goods.

45

Settlers rode the new railway west to Alberta.

the National Policy. The National Policy had three main points: high tariffs on imported goods to protect Canadian manufacturers, the completion of the **transcontinental** railway through Canada, and an increased emphasis on immigration to help populate the West.

Canadians had forgiven Macdonald for the Pacific scandal. He had a **charismatic** style, and those who turned out to hear him speak came away excited. Mackenzie, on the other hand, was a serious man who prided himself on his honesty. He told Canadians, truthfully, that the economy was bad and showed no signs of improvement. They preferred Macdonald's **optimism**.

Macdonald and the Conservatives swept into power again in the election of 1878. People loved the National Policy. Even though western Canadians had their doubts about raising the tariffs, they badly wanted a railway connecting them to the rest of Canada. Those in Ontario and Québec did not care as much about the railway, but they liked the protective tariffs. Most agreed that settling the prairies was a good idea. The National Policy had something for everyone to like.

The National Policy remained in effect for many years, but after the railway was completed the policy lost its appeal in the West. High import tariffs meant western Canadians were restricted to buying expensive Canadian goods from back east, rather than cheaper goods from just over the American border.

Macdonald's second stretch of time as prime minister of Canada was marked by the construction and completion of the Canadian Pacific Railway. These years would also see the return of Louis Riel, who would come back to Canada to lead an even more violent rebellion.

*Something that is **transcontinental** crosses an entire continent.*

*Someone who is **charismatic** has great powers of charm or influence.*

***Optimism** is a hopeful, positive attitude that expects events to turn out for the best.*

The battle at Duck Lake

Four

TRIUMPHS AND TURMOIL

Near Duck Lake, the snow crunched underfoot as the four men walked toward each other, two from each opposing force. Behind them, on either side, the Métis moved into position behind trees, while the force of English settlers and NWMP took cover behind their sleighs.

The men on both sides feared treachery. They wanted to negotiate, but at the same time, no one trusted anyone else. Carrying his rifle in his arms, Gentleman Joe McKay, interpreter and guide for the NWMP, stood next to Superintendent Leif Crozier. McKay held out his hand to one of the two men, a Cree who had accompanied Isidore Dumont of the Métis. The Cree, thinking McKay was preparing to shoot, grabbed the barrel of the gun and tried to wrestle it away. McKay pulled out a pistol and fired. Chaos broke out. Both Isidore Dumont and the Cree fell dead in the road. Crozier and McKay retreated to the shelter of the sleighs.

Despite the NWMP's greater numbers, the Métis were able to push them back. Half an hour later, twelve police officers and settlers had been killed, along with six Métis. Throughout the battle, Louis Riel, unprotected from the flying bullets, rode back and forth behind his men, waving a crucifix and shouting encouragement.

The North-West Rebellion

After the Red River Rebellion, Louis Riel had fled to the United States. The people of Manitoba, especially the Métis, still considered him a hero, though, and twice elected him to the House of Commons. In 1875, Prime Minister Alexander Mackenzie had pardoned Riel, but under the terms of the pardon, he was exiled from Canada for five years.

In the years that followed, Riel suffered from depression and occasional bouts of delusions. He spent time in several insane asylums, but gradually recovered. In 1884, he was living quietly in Montana, working as a school teacher. He had married and had two young children.

By the 1880s, most of the Métis had left the Red River area and moved west into the Northwest Territories, to what is now cen-

Métis prisoners during the North-West Rebellion of 1885

tral Saskatchewan. Many English-speaking settlers had moved to the area as well, and the Métis felt crowded. They wanted a place of their own, a French-Catholic Métis province. Wherever they moved, English settlers moved as well. The Canadian government would not listen to the Métis' complaints. Riel, the Métis said to each other, was the only man who could help them.

In the summer of 1884, a delegation of Métis arrived at Riel's home in Montana to ask him to return to Canada and lead the Métis once more. Riel took this as a sign from God. He had grown to think of himself as the prophet of the Métis, destined to give

his people freedom and a new homeland. He returned with the delegation to the Métis community of Batoche.

Riel gathered a council of Métis and put together a petition to send to Prime Minister Macdonald. The petition requested the Métis be given their own province, with an elected government and control over their own land. Macdonald took a long time to respond, but he finally sent word that he would think about the idea. He promised to put together a committee to look into the situation.

The Métis did not like Macdonald's answer at all. They wanted something done quickly, not put aside to think about for years. On March 19, 1885, Riel formed a provisional government. He hoped to force the Canadian government to meet Métis demands.

On March 26, nearly one hundred NWMP officers and English settlers rode out to meet the Métis rebels. They clashed at Duck Lake, the first battle of the North-West Rebellion. Although the Métis were severely outnumbered, they won the Battle of Duck Lake. Their advantage, however, did not last long. By May, they were running out of both food and ammunition. On May 15, Riel surrendered.

The Death of Louis Riel

Riel pleaded not guilty to the charge of *treason* and was tried by a jury of English-speaking Protestants. He refused to plead

Louis Riel

What Time Is It?

In the days before railways, people figured out the time by looking at the sun. With quicker travel by train, though, this system became confusing. Train schedules were difficult to follow, since the time at one end of the route would be different than at the other end. In the 1870s, Sir Sandford Fleming, a Scottish immigrant to Canada who worked as the supervising engineer on the Canadian Pacific Railway, devised a standardized world clock, divided into twenty-four time zones. The idea of time zones was not new, but the idea of standardizing these zones all over the world originated with Fleming. By the 1920s, most of the world had accepted Fleming's system of Universal Standard Time.

insanity, although his lawyer advised him against that decision. The jury found Riel guilty, but recommended he be given mercy. The judge ignored their advice and sentenced Riel to death.

The Métis and many French Canadians asked Prime Minister Macdonald to intervene and save Riel from execution, but Macdonald refused. A lot of people felt Riel was being executed because of the death of Thomas Scott, a crime Alexander Mackenzie had pardoned ten years earlier.

On November 16, 1885, Louis Riel was hanged for treason. With his death, he became a figure of legend—hero to some, villain to others. Over one hundred years after his execution, some still believe he was wrongly executed. They see his trial

Treason is the betrayal of one's country.

and execution as a symbol of racial struggle—Métis against Canadian, French against English.

Finishing the Canadian Pacific Railway

When Sir John A. Macdonald became prime minister again in 1878, he negotiated with several businesspeople and hired Andrew Onderdonk to run the Canadian Pacific Railway Company and build the transcontinental railway in Canada. Building as quickly and as cheaply as possible—with the cost of hundreds of lives, many of them Chinese—much progress had been made. By 1885, however the railway was still not finished, and money was running out. The company was deeply in debt and in danger

Driving the last spike

of bankruptcy. The project faltered and work slowed.

When the North-West Rebellion broke out in the spring of 1885, the railway company suggested the government transport military reinforcements west by train. Though not all sections had been completed, the railway speeded the journey greatly. The trip took nine days instead of the more than three months it would have taken without the railway.

The success of the Canadian Pacific Railway in ending the North-West Rebellion quickly showed Canadians how useful the railway could be. Until Riel returned, a cross-Canada railway had begun to seem unnecessary to the Canadian government. Prompted by the rebellion, Macdonald gave the company a massive loan to finish the project, and work continued. On November 7, 1885, the last spike was driven in at Craigellachie, British Columbia. The next June, the first cross-country train left Montréal, making the journey in less than a week. The transcontinental railway was complete.

The Death of Sir John A. Macdonald

In the general election of 1891, Macdonald ran again as the Conservative Party candi-

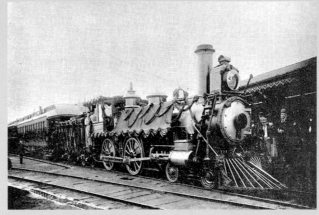

Macdonald's funeral train

date for prime minister. He was seventy-six years old and had served as prime minister of Canada for nineteen years. He campaigned on the principles of the National Policy that had won him the election of 1878—minus the completion of the railway—and denounced his Liberal opponent when he brought up free trade with the United States.

Macdonald won the election, which was in March. The people liked "the old man," as he called himself, and his policies had worked for Canada so far.

Two months later, on May 29, Macdonald had a stroke. He was worn out from his long battle with alcoholism and from the stress of leading the country for so long. For over a week, he clung to life, unable to speak. On the evening of June 6, Sir John A. Macdonald, first prime minister of Canada and Father of Confederation, died. Thousands of Canadians turned out for his funeral, and thousands more lined the tracks as the black-draped funeral train carried his body from Ottawa to his hometown of Kingston, Ontario, for burial.

Political Upheaval

Macdonald had been a strong leader for Canada. The Conservative Party was not prepared for his death and had no one lined up to take his place immediately. For ten days, the office of prime minister sat vacant while the Conservative Party scrambled to find a replacement.

One of the top politicians in the Conservative Party at the time was John Sparrow Thompson, but Thompson was a Roman Catholic, and many Canadians did not like Catholics. Finally, the party was able to convince John Abbot to take the office of prime minister. Abbot was a Senator and had formerly served as a Member of Parliament and as mayor of Montréal. Though Abbot did not want to be prime minister, he agreed to take the job if Thompson would help him with many of the responsibilities.

John Sparrow Thompson

Despite his reluctance to become prime minister, Abbot worked hard to do a good job. Canadians liked him, and he kept their confidence in the Conservative Party. After just over a year in office, however, Abbot became ill. He was over seventy, and being prime minister had exhausted him physically and mentally. His doctors told him he needed a long rest.

On December 5, 1892, John Abbot resigned as prime minister, and John Sparrow Thompson took over. Even though many Canadians did not approve of his religion, no one else could be found who would be able to run the country. Abbot died less than a year later, and Thompson served as prime minister for two years.

On December 12, 1894, Thompson was in Great Britain. Queen Victoria had just made him a member of her Privy Council, a group of her advisers. Then, suddenly, the forty-nine-year-old Thompson suffered a heart attack and died. Again, Canada was left with no prime minister.

The highest member of the Conservative Party was Mackenzie Bowell, leader of the government in the Senate. Bowell took office as prime minister nine days after Thompson's death. Bowell was very happy to be prime minister, but the rest of the Conservative Party was not so sure about him. He was an old man and set in his ways. Without a strong leader in its midst, the Conservative Party membership was becoming increasingly split. Finally, facing a

Mackenzie Bowell

Charles Tupper

*A **cabinet** is a governing official's group of advisers.*

***Radical** involves extensive, often quick, changes.*

"nest of traitors," as he said, in his own **cabinet**, Bowell resigned after a little more than a year as prime minister.

Charles Tupper replaced Mackenzie Bowell on May 1, 1896. Tupper was seventy-four years old, the oldest Canadian to take office as prime minister. He had been the Father of Confederation in Nova Scotia, ushering that province into the union with Canada in 1867.

The Manitoba Schools Question

A general election was scheduled for June, and Tupper needed to work hard to convince Canadians the Conservative Party was still able to lead Canada. Opposing him was a younger man, a French Canadian who had managed to win many supporters in Québec, Wilfred Laurier of the Liberal Party. The Conservative Party counted on votes from Québec, where Liberals and their **radical** ideals were traditionally

Manitoba's prairie land

scorned. Laurier, however, was much more conservative than most Liberal candidates. He did not argue for free trade with the United States, an issue that had lost the Liberals the last several elections. Instead, Laurier supported the National Policy, the great innovation of Sir John A. Macdonald.

The major issue of the election of 1896 was the Manitoba Schools Question. In 1870, when Manitoba had become a province, the Manitoba Act had ensured that the province would be bilingual and had promised separate schools for English Protestants and for French Catholics. At the time, the numbers of English- and French-speakers in Manitoba had been nearly equal. By 1890, English-speaking settlers far outnumbered the French, and the Manitoba government passed the Manitoba Schools Act, making English the official language of the province and taking all funding away from the French-Catholic schools. French Canadians believed the province should not be able to go against the Manitoba Act in this way.

Canadians were very divided on the Manitoba Schools Question. The issue dealt with minority rights, but also with provincial rights—whether the provinces could change laws written by the federal government. Prime Minister Tupper and the Conservative Party supported the original Manitoba Act and the minority rights of the French Catholics, even though many Conservative politicians personally disliked Roman Catholics. Tupper believed that because the Manitoba Act had promised separate schools, these schools must be maintained, even though very few French Catholics might live in the area. Laurier, speaking for the Liberals, did not say exactly what he planned to do if he were elected, but did promise to resolve the issue and to use compromises to make as many people as possible happy.

When Canadians voted on June 23, 1896, they chose the Liberals to lead the country. Wilfred Laurier became the first French Canadian prime minister and the first Liberal prime minister since Alexander Mackenzie eighteen years before. Charles

Wilfred Laurier

Tupper had served as prime minister for only a little more than two months.

As soon as Laurier took office on July 11, 1896, he focused on solving the Manitoba Schools Question. In November, he agreed on a compromise with Thomas Greenway, the premier of Manitoba. The Laurier-Greenway Compromise did not restore separate schools. Instead, there would be half an hour at the end of each school day devoted to religious instruction, Catholic or Protestant. If at least ten students in a district were French-speaking, school would be taught in both French and English; otherwise, education would be only in English. The same rule applied to those speaking other languages; so if, for example, a large number of German-speakers attended a certain school, they could be taught in both German and English.

Many French Catholics were very opposed to the Laurier-Greenway Compromise. They felt it did not go far enough to meet the needs of the French-Catholic minority in Manitoba. They appealed to Pope Leo XIII and asked him to talk to Prime Minister Laurier on their behalf. In response, the pope sent someone to Canada to investigate the complaint. The Catholic Church concluded that Laurier had made the best possible compromise in the situation.

Settlers moving west

The election of Wilfred Laurier brought Canada into a new era of Liberal leadership. For years, Sir John A. Macdonald and the Conservative Party led Canada. With Macdonald's death in office in 1891, the Conservative Party found itself in crisis, trying to quickly find someone to fill the office. The four prime ministers who followed in the five years after Macdonald's death all served as interim prime ministers, since none of them had been officially elected. By the time an election was held in 1896, the Conservative Party had been splintered and divided by the frequent turnover in leadership and by the Manitoba Schools Question.

Laurier and the Liberals would lead Canada for the next fifteen years. During the Laurier years, the prairies would fill with immigrants. Drawing them was the promise of nearly free land. In the northwest, newly discovered gold would also set off one of the last gold rushes in North America.

Gold prospectors

Five

RUSHING THE WEST

On August 16, 1896, Skookum Jim, his sister Kate, and Kate's husband, George Carmack, along with several other First Nations men, were camped on Rabbit Creek, a tributary of the Klondike River. They had been prospecting for gold in the region for several weeks. Then, someone picked up a loose stone. Underneath was the unmistakable gleam of gold! The nugget was small, but the party was encouraged. With new energy, they searched for loose rock. It came away in sheets, and below was more gold than they had ever imagined, lying thick between the layers of stone.

"It looks like a cheese sandwich," Carmack said with awe. One of the other men renamed the creek Bonanza.

The Klondike Gold Rush

When Skookum Jim and George Carmack found gold near the Klondike, they set off a major gold rush, although the news took nearly a year to filter south. The Klondike area was in the western part of the huge Northwest Territories of Canada, just over the border from Alaska in what would soon become the Yukon Territory.

One hundred thousand prospectors rushed to the Klondike region from across Canada and the United States. In Canada,

Newspaper headlines broadcast the news of gold.

thousands of NWMP officers also rushed to keep order and bring the law to the chaos of the mining camps. The close involvement of the NWMP made the Klondike gold rush one of the most orderly in history. It made sure the theft and brawling that went on among the gold-hungry prospectors was kept to a minimum.

Most American prospectors arrived by way of Alaska, climbing the steep passes overland into Canada. Prospectors were required to bring a year's worth of goods with them into Canada, a load weighing nearly a ton. NWMP officers patrolled the border into Canada, turning away those who had not brought the necessary supplies and were not prepared to face the cold and snow of the north.

Prospectors had to make the trip over Chilkoot Pass into Canada lugging all their equipment. The last half mile (four-fifths of a kilometer) of the trail soared a thousand feet (over 300 meters) nearly straight up. Prospectors climbed the narrow trail in single file, up steps cut into the ice, clutching a guide rope with their supplies strapped to their backs. The trip took two hours. At the top, they dropped off their packs, slid down the hill sitting on their shovels, and picked up another load to carry.

After facing extreme cold, sheer mountain passes, and the backbreaking work of hauling their supplies hundreds of miles across rough terrain, most prospectors finally arrived on the Klondike gold fields to discover the best claims had been snapped

Communication Across the Miles

In the early days of Canadian history, communicating with distant towns was slow and difficult. Letters took a long time to arrive. By the late nineteenth century, certain inventions made communicating across the miles far quicker. With the completion of the cross-Canada railway, letters could travel much faster. Then, in 1866, a telegraph cable connecting North America with Europe was laid down across the Atlantic Ocean. Telegraph messages in Morse code could be sent quickly along the cable. In the 1870s, Alexander Graham Bell, a Scottish immigrant, patented his telephone, and soon telephones were appearing everywhere, revolutionizing communications yet again. In 1901, from atop what would be named Signal Hill in St. John's, Newfoundland, Guglielmo Marconi sent the first radio transmission. Wireless signals meant telegraphs could be sent without the enormous expense of stringing wires. Little by little, Canada and the world grew closer together as communications became quicker and easier.

To deal with the increased population, the Canadian government moved quickly to bring greater government control to the region. In July of 1898, Canada passed the Yukon Act, creating the Yukon Territory out of the larger Northwest Territories. Instead of being led by a premier, as the provinces

Klondike prospectors

Clifford Sifton, minister of the interior, worked to bring immigrants west.

up the year before. Many arrived, saw the crowds, and left for home. Others stayed and gave up their dream of gold to instead get rich selling equipment or services to the prospectors. Only a very few became rich on gold.

The town of Dawson City grew up, on the site of a First Nations fishing camp, its population ballooning to nearly thirty thousand by 1898. From nothing at all, a modern town, with electricity and motion picture theaters, appeared in the wilderness.

Immigrants from Ukraine

were, an appointed commissioner would oversee the government in the Yukon.

When the frenzy of the gold rush ended in 1899, the population dropped dramatically as prospectors returned to their homes. Most gold miners left in the next few years, but some chose to stay in the Yukon, finding they loved the harsh but beautiful land.

Immigrants to the West

While the Northwest and the Yukon Territories were being populated by the gold rush, Canada was working hard to attract settlers to the wide-open prairie land. The Dominion Lands Act of 1872 had been aimed at increasing western settlers, but not many people responded for several decades. The completion of the railway in 1885 helped make the journey west easier, and the Canadian government had acquired large amounts of First Nations land through the Numbered Treaties, which opened up more land for settlement.

In 1896, Clifford Sifton, the Canadian minister of the interior, launched an aggressive advertising campaign to entice immigrants to Canada. Sifton set up offices in Europe and the United States and sent out posters and brochures describing the wonders of the Canadian West. "The Last Best West," the posters announced. "Homes for Millions."

A lot of people thought of the West as a barren, bleak place, with cold winds screaming across empty lands. Sifton's campaign worked hard to change that image. He

A Ukranian farmer on his homestead in Alberta

wanted people across the world to think of the Canadian prairies as a rich, fertile place. Snow and cold were not mentioned at all in the advertising brochures. Instead, Sifton offered 180 acres (almost 73 hectares) of free land in an invigorating environment.

Sifton's ideal immigrant was a hardworking farmer, preferably from northern Europe or the United States. He feared people from southern regions, or those not used to hard labor, would not be able to survive the long, harsh Canadian winters on the prairies.

Over the next few decades, several million immigrants entered Canada, drawn by the promise of free land and a new life. Some left their home countries to escape religious persecution, while others had found the increasing populations in Europe made it very difficult to find farmland to support their families.

Many of the immigrants came from Great Britain and the United States, but many also arrived from Ukraine, and others came from Scandinavia and from across Europe. Once they made the long journey by boat across the Atlantic Ocean, they had to board trains to take them west to the prairies. The voyage could be frightening and exhausting for immigrants as they arrived in a land where nothing was familiar, not even the language.

Once the immigrants reached their destinations and had been assigned plots of land, they faced the task of building houses and turning the property into productive farms. The climate was harsh, not all the land was fertile, and sometimes there were droughts,

Settlers' tent camp in Saskatchewan

floods, or grasshoppers. Some immigrants were not used to farming, and those who had farmed in their home countries usually were used to hillier, more wooded areas. Nearly a third of those who started farming on the Canadian prairies gave up. Some moved to the cities, where the speed of life better suited them. A few went home, missing their home countries too much to stay.

While the Canadian government wanted people to come to Canada and farm on the prairies, they did not want just anyone. Clifford Sifton had in mind a certain type of immigrant, and those from Great Britain or northern Europe best suited his ideal. He would accept those from eastern or southern Europe, but those he wanted least of all were blacks and Asians. Some Canadians

even thought Sifton was being far too open to allow so many Ukrainians, Germans, and Scandinavians to settle in the West. They wanted to keep Canada more British.

A number of Chinese immigrants had settled in British Columbia in the middle of the nineteenth century when many Chinese men had worked to help build the Canadian Pacific Railway. In 1885, Canada introduced a tax on Chinese immigrants, hoping to discourage them from immigrating. The Chinese who did come to Canada worked at the lowest-paying, most dangerous jobs. Nineteenth-century Canadians did not like to think of the Chinese as permanent additions to the population of Canada, but instead as short-term workers for hard labor.

Clifford Sifton's campaign to attract immigrants worked. In 1891, the population of the prairies was approximately 250,000, only 5 percent of the total population of Canada. Thirty years later, the prairie population had leaped to almost two million, 22 percent of the total population.

Homes for Orphans

In the late nineteenth century, thousands of orphaned children from Great Britain found homes in Canada. Dr. Barnardo's homes, refuges for orphans and street children begun by Thomas John Barnardo in London, sent shiploads of children from the overcrowded institutions in Great Britain to Canada and Australia. Though a few of these children were adopted, most worked on farms or as servants. Most of these children thrived in their new lives, away from the London slums where they had been born.

Captain Bernier on board the Artic *with a First Nations man*

With so many people moving into the West, Prime Minister Laurier decided to create two new provinces out of the Northwest Territories. The Autonomy Acts of 1905 brought the provinces of Saskatchewan and Alberta into Confederation. These provinces bridged the land between Manitoba and British Columbia.

The Northern Frontier

In the late nineteenth century, Canada divided the Northwest Territories into several administrative districts. After the creation of the Yukon Territory in 1898 and the new provinces of Alberta and Saskatchewan in 1905, the remaining districts were the

The Arctic Archipelago

District of Mackenzie to the east of the Yukon, the District of Keewatin north of Manitoba, and the District of Franklin in the far north.

Despite Canada's claims on the northern regions, nobody even knew for certain how many islands lay in the Arctic *Archipelago*. The northern islands had never been officially claimed, only included in a general claim of the entire area.

In 1908, Joseph-Élzear Bernier, a Québec-born sea captain, convinced Prime Minister Laurier to fund an expedition to the North to formally claim each island for Canada. Bernier set out from Québec City on July 28, 1908, in his ship the Arctic. For the rest of the summer, Bernier and his crew sailed from island to island, claiming them for Canada. At each island, Bernier would climb a hill and bury a metal box under a *cairn* of stones. Inside the box was the proclamation of Canada's claim on the region. Then he would put up the Canadian flag—identical to Great Britain's at this point.

Bernier spent the winter in the Arctic, and, by the next year, he had claimed all the islands he knew. Finally, on July 1, 1909, he put up a bronze plaque on Melville Island, celebrating the success of his expedition. The plaque read, "This memorial is erected today to commemorate the taking possession for the Dominion of Canada of the whole Arctic Archipelago."

Even with Bernier's claims, the ownership of the Arctic Archipelago was not completely settled. In the 1930s, a Canadian pilot would make an aerial survey of the Arctic, reinforcing Canada's claims on the area. In 1931, Norway gave up its claims in the region, but controversy with the United States over who controls the water between the islands of the Arctic Archipelago continues to this day.

*An **archipelago** is a group or chain of islands.*

*A **cairn** is a pile of stones used as a marker.*

A stone cairn in Canada's far north

Canada's North

When Canada became a country in 1867, it had consisted only of four provinces in the east—Ontario, Québec, New Brunswick, and Nova Scotia. Quickly, the country grew, with the purchase of the vast reaches of Rupert's Land and the North-Western Territory in 1869. British Columbia joined Confederation in 1871, and Canada then spread from the Atlantic to the Pacific.

With Bernier's voyage to officially claim the islands of the Arctic, Canada now stretched to the farthest reaches of the North. In less than fifty years, Canada had grown from a small country, with a population of around three and a half million, to an immense land touching the shores of three oceans, with a population of nearly seven million. The physical shape of Canada was nearly complete; the last piece, the island of Newfoundland and the coast of Labrador, would not be added until 1949.

In the next twenty years, the issues Canada would face would not be those of physical growth or the challenge to attract immigrants. Instead, Canada would wrestle with questions of sovereignty, especially in the face of the world war that would soon explode in Europe. Canada was a country, but it was still not fully independent from Britain where international matters were concerned. That relationship would be tested in the years to come.

1867 The United States purchases Alaska from Russia.

1763 Royal Proclamation of 1763 guarantees First Nations rights to all land west of the settled eastern regions.

December 1, 1869 Red River becomes essentially independent.

1870s The Numbered Treaties are signed with the First Nations of the Plains.

1867 Canada becomes a country.

March 4, 1870 Thomas Scott is executed by firing squad.

July 1871 Dominion Lands Survey starts.

1872 Canada passes the Dominion Lands Act.

July 15, 1870 The Manitoba Act gives Canada control of Rupert's Land and the North-Western Territory, and Manitoba becomes a province.

July 20, 1871 British Columbia joins Canada.

July 1, 1873 Prince Edward Island joins Canada.

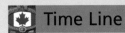

1885 North-West Rebellion breaks out.

1874 Prime Minister Mackenzie introduces the secret ballot method of voting.

November 7, 1885 The transcontinental railway is completed.

2638

November 16, 1885 Louis Riel is hanged for treason.

1875 Prime Minister Mackenzie creates the Supreme Court of Canada.

June 23, 1896 Wilfred Laurier becomes the first French Canadian prime minister.

1905 Autonomy Acts of 1905 bring Saskatchewan and Alberta into Confederation.

July 1898 Canada passes the Yukon Act.

1949 Newfoundland and the coast of Labrador join Canada.

1901 Guglielmo Marconi sends first radio transmission from Signal Hill.

FURTHER READING

Berton, Pierre. *Bonanza Gold: The Great Klondike Gold Rush*. Toronto, Ont.: McClelland & Stewart, 1991.

Berton, Pierre. *The Men in Sheepskin Coats*. Toronto, Ont.: McClelland & Stewart, 1992.

Berton, Pierre. *The Railway Pathfinders: Canada Moves West*. Grand Rapids, Mich.: Zondervan Publishing House, 1995.

Hamilton-Barry, Joann. *Boldly Canadian: The Story of the Royal Canadian Mounted Police*. Toronto, Ont.: Kids Can Press, 1999.

MacLeod, Elizabeth. *Alexander Graham Bell: An Inventive Life*. Toronto, Ont.: Kids Can Press, 1999.

Neering, Rosemary. *Louis Riel*. Markham, Ont.: Fitzhenry & Whiteside, 1998.

Peacock, Shane. *Unusual Heroes: Canada's Prime Ministers and Fathers of Confederation*. Toronto, Ont.: Penguin Books, 2002.

Quan, Holly. *Native Chiefs and Famous Métis: Leadership and Bravery in the Canadian West*. Canmore, Alb.: Altitude Publishing, 2003.

Ward, Donald. *The People: A Historical Guide to the First Nations of Alberta, Saskatchewan, and Manitoba*. Markham, Ont.: Fitzhenry & Whiteside, 1995.

Webb, Michael. *Sandford Fleming: Railway Builder*. Mississauga, Ont.: Copp Clark Pitman, 1993.

FOR MORE INFORMATION

Advertising for Immigrants
www.civilization.ca/hist/advertis/
ads1-01e.html

Canada in the Making
www.canadiana.org/citm/index_e.html

Canadian Confederation
www.collectionscanada.ca/confederation/
h18-2100-e.html

Canadian Pacific Railway History
www.cprheritage.com/history/display1.htm

The First Shot Rang Out, Duck Lake
Interpretive Center
www.virtualmuseum.ca/
pm.php?id=exhibit_home&fl=0&lg=
English&ex=00000134

Klondike Gold Rush, The Perilous
Journey North
www.lib.washington.edu/specialcoll/
klondike/index.html

Sir John A. Macdonald
www.canadahistory.com/sections/
politics/PRIMEMINISTERS/
John_A_Macdonald.htm

The Peopling of Canada, 1891–1921
www.ucalgary.ca/applied_history/tutor/
canada1891/

RCMP History
www.rcmpgrc.gc.ca/history/history_e.htm

Louis Riel, the Heritage Center of
Saint-Boniface
www.shsb.mb.ca/Riel/indexenglish.htm

Publisher's note:
The Web sites listed on this page were active at the time of publication. The publisher is not responsible for Web sites that have changed their addresses or discontinued operation since the date of publication. The publisher will review and update the Web-site list upon each reprint.

INDEX

PICTURE CREDITS

Benjamin Stewart: pp. 74, 76

Canada Department of Foreign Affairs and International Trade: p. 41 (left)

Canadian Illustrated News: p. 44

Hudson's Bay Company Archives, Provincial Archives of Manitoba: pp. 8–9

Metropolitan Toronto Reference Library: p. 40

National Archives of Canada: pp. 10, 11, 13, 14 (right), 15, 16, 17, 18–19, 21, 24–25, 26–27, 34–35, 38, 41 (right), 42–43, 45, 46, 50–51, 54, 56, 57, 60, 61, 66 (right), 67, 68–69, 70–71, 73, 78–79, 80–81

Norm Kerychuk: p. 29

Photos.com: pp. 1, 20, 22, 36–37, 58–59

University of Manitoba Library: p. 14 (left)

World Wildlife Fund: pp. 30–31

To the best knowledge of the publisher, all other images are in the public domain. If any image has been inadvertently uncredited, please notify Harding House Publishing Service, Vestal, New York 13850, so that rectification can be made for future printings.

BIOGRAPHIES

Sheila Nelson was born in Newfoundland and grew up in both Newfoundland and Ontario. She has written a number of history books for kids and always enjoys the chance to keep learning. She recently earned a master's degree and now lives in Rochester, New York, with her husband and daughter.

SERIES CONSULTANT

Dr. David Bercuson is the Director of the Centre for Military and Strategic Studies at the University of Calgary. His writings on modern Canadian politics, Canadian defense and foreign policy, and Canadian military, among other topics, have appeared in academic and popular publications. Dr. Bercuson is the author, coauthor, or editor of more than thirty books, including *Confrontation at Winnipeg: Labour, Industrial Relations, and the General Strike* (1990), *Colonies: Canada to 1867* (1992), *Maple Leaf Against the Axis, Canada's Second World War* (1995), and *Christmas in Washington: Roosevelt and Churchill Forge the Alliance* (2005). He has also served as historical consultant for several film and television projects, and provided political commentary for CBC radio and television and CTV television. In 1989, Dr. Bercuson was elected a fellow of the Royal Society of Canada. In 2004, Dr. Bercuson received the Vimy Award, sponsored by the Conference of Defence Association Institute, in recognition of his significant contributions to Canada's defense and the preservation of the Canadian democratic principles.